My "d" Sound Box®

WRITTEN BY JANE BELK MONCURE • ILLUSTRATED BY REBECCA THORNBURGH

The Child's World®
childsworld.com

Published by The Child's World®
1980 Lookout Drive • Mankato, MN 56003-1705
800-599-READ • www.childsworld.com

ISBN HARDCOVER: 9781503823075
ISBN PAPERBACK: 9781503831292
LCCN: 2017960288

Printed in the United States of America
PA02371

A NOTE TO PARENTS AND EDUCATORS:

Magic moon machines and five fat frogs are just a few of the fun things you can share with children by reading books with them. Reading aloud helps children in so many ways! It introduces them to new words, motivates them to develop their own reading skills, and expands their attention span and listening abilities. So it's important to find time each day to share a book or two . . . or three!

As you read with young children, you can help develop their understanding of how print works by talking about the parts of the book—the cover, the title, the illustrations, and the words that tell the story. As you read, use your finger to point to each word, modeling a gentle sweep from left to right.

Simple word games help develop important prereading skills, including an understanding of rhyme and alliteration (when words share the same beginning sound, such as "six" and "sand"). Try playing with words from a book you've just shared: "What other words start with the same sound as moon?" "Cat and hat, do those words rhyme?" The possibilities are endless—and so are the rewards!

My "d" Sound Box®

Little  had a box. "I will find things that begin with my **d** sound," she said.

"I will put them into my sound box."

Little  found dolls.

She found all kinds of dolls.

Dolls, dolls, dolls!

One doll danced.

One doll played a drum.

Did Little  put the dolls into her box? She did.

But some dolls fell out.

So Little  said, "I will turn this box into a dollhouse for the dolls and me!"

And she did.

Little  made doll desks and doll dressers.

She put them in the dollhouse.

She made a dining room with a table.

She put dishes on the table.

Little  made doll dresses.

She made all kinds of doll dresses.

Then she dressed her dolls . . .

and took them for a drive in the desert.

Little  made some toys for her dolls.

She made ducks for some dolls.

She made dogs for some dolls. She put

the ducks and dogs into the dollhouse.

One day, a doll was sick.

So Little  took the doll to a doctor.

One day, a doll had a toothache.

So Little  took the doll to a dentist.

One day, Little  opened the door

and found a dollar and a dime.

"I will buy some donuts for my dolls," she said.

"We will have donuts for dinner."

She put a dozen donuts on the dining room table.

Why did she need a dozen?

Little 's Word List

dentist

dishes

donut

desert

doctor

door

desk

dog

dress

dime

doll

dresser

dining room

dollar

drum

dinner

dollhouse

duck

Other Words with Little

daisy

dandelion

deer

diamond

diaper

diary

dice

dinosaur

doghouse

dolphin

domino

donkey

dove

dragonfly

dustpan

More to Do!

Little  created a dollhouse for her dolls. You can create your own dollhouse with a little help from an adult.

What you need:

- old magazines and catalogs
- an empty cereal or tissue box
- construction paper
- scissors
- glue

Directions:

1. Use your scissors to cut construction-paper pieces that will cover all sides of the box (inside and out). Glue the paper to the box. This will be your dollhouse.

2. Now look through the magazines and catalogs for pictures. How many things can you find that begin with the letter **d**? What did you find that you could put in your dollhouse? A desk? A door?

3. Decorate your dollhouse with all the **d** things you find. Maybe you will find a doll with a dimple, or dishes with dots!

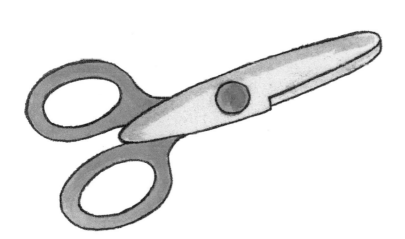

GOOEY GLUE

About the Author

Best-selling author Jane Belk Moncure (1926–2013) wrote more than 300 books throughout her teaching and writing career. After earning a master's degree in early childhood education from Columbia University, she became one of the pioneers in that field. In 1956, she helped form the Virginia Association for Early Childhood Education, which established the first statewide standards for teachers of young children.

Inspired by her work in the classroom, Mrs. Moncure's books became standards in primary education, and her name was recognized across the country. Her success was reflected not only in her books' popularity with parents, children, and educators, but also by numerous awards, including the 1984 C. S. Lewis Gold Medal Award.

About the Illustrator

Rebecca Thornburgh lives in a pleasantly spooky old house in Philadelphia. If she's not at her drawing table, she's reading—or singing with her band, called Reckless Amateurs. Rebecca has one husband, two daughters, and two silly dogs.